ORVILLE

Clarion Books
a Houghton Mifflin Company imprint
215 Park Avenue South, New York, NY 10003
Text copyright © 2003 by Haven Kimmel
Illustrations copyright © 2003 by Robert Andrew Parker

The illustrations were executed in watercolor and ink.
The text was set in 14-point Garamond Book Condensed.

www.houghtonmifflinbooks.com

Printed in Singapore

Library of Congress Cataloging-in-Publication Data

Kimmel, Haven
Orville / by Haven Kimmel; illustrated by Robert Andrew Parker.
p. cm.
Summary: Chained alone in a barn by the couple he thought might give him
a good home, a very ugly stray dog is miserable until a new neighbor
moves in and he falls in love.
ISBN 0-618-15955-X
[1. Dogs—Fiction. 2. Human-animal relationships—Fiction.
3. Farm life—Fiction.] I. Parker, Robert Andrew, ill. II. Title.
PZ7.K56483 Or 2003   [E]—dc21   2002155649
TWP   10 9 8 7 6 5 4 3 2 1

For Obadiah
and
For All The Good Dogs
—H. K.

For my brother Bill
—R. A. P.

ORVILLE

A Dog Story

by Haven Kimmel

Illustrated by Robert Andrew Parker

CLARION BOOKS • NEW YORK

He was so lost, and had been lost
for so long, that when the early April
thunderstorm blew in like a freight train,
the dog lay down in the culvert,
covered his eyes with his paws,
and decided to never get up again.

All night he lay wet and shivering.
In the morning the sun broke through the clouds,
brighter and warmer than he'd seen it for months,
and he forgot he had vowed to never rise again,
and rose and stretched.
He stretched all of his legs, his tail, and his belly.
He even opened his mouth and stretched out
his tongue, and when he did,
a little morning squeak came out of his mouth
and made him jump.

Just as the dog finished stretching,
a farmer and his wife came
around the curve in the gravel road,
kicking up dust.
The dog thought he'd like to say hello
to them, and wouldn't it be fine
just to say hello. But he couldn't exactly
remember which bark was "Hello"
and which was "Run for your life!"
And when he started barking,
there was a lot mixed up in it,
including how he'd love
to have some breakfast,
and hasn't this been a miserably
cold winter.

The farmer backed up a step, or maybe it
was five or six, but the woman walked
right up to the dog and offered him
her hand. The dog smelled it,
and this is what he learned:
She could make a perfect pan of biscuits.
Her name was Maybelle, but everyone called her
May. Her sister had died young,
which had broken May's heart.
Her dearest wishes were, in order:
To fly a little airplane.
To lead a parade.
To serve as the sheriff of a small town.

The dog became so excited he began to run
in circles, and then he thought,
"Wouldn't it be nice just to jump right up
on her," but remembered the part
about knocking people down and so he didn't.
"That's the ugliest dog I've ever seen,"
the farmer said, and the look on his face said
he truly meant it.
"He's ugly, all right," Maybelle said, "and
half-starved, too. I'm thinking we should
take him home. He'd make a good watchdog,
and maybe he could run the rats out of the barn."

9

The dog stopped running. He smelled a picture
in the air of rats and barns,
and he didn't take kindly to the notion.
The farmer thought a minute,
then whistled, and against the dog's own
best judgment he galloped over to the farmer
and smelled his boots and pants and hands.
And it wasn't the worst news in the world,
but it wasn't the best:
The farmer's name was Herbert.
He worked hard but always forgot
what he was working for.
He didn't appreciate a good joke.
He often said, "I don't live to eat, I eat to live,
so just put the food on my plate."
His dearest wishes:
A good night's sleep.
An uneventful harvest.
A big green tractor with a radio in the cab.

Maybelle and Herbert called the dog
Orville, but that was not his real name.
He had forgotten all of it except a "k" sound
at the beginning and something in the middle
that sounded like "no."
There had been other people, too,
whose smells gave their whole lives away,
but he had left them.
There were some things he remembered
(a leaky doghouse at the edge of a muddy yard,
a little girl who carried a one-eyed doll),
but mostly he tried to forget.
Everywhere he had ever lived involved a chain,
and he had broken every one,
and there were six spots on his neck
where hair didn't grow
because the chains had rubbed it off.

Orville went to live at the farmer's house,
and after he'd been cleaned up a bit
Maybelle and Herbert realized he was uglier
than they'd thought when he was dirty.
He was taller than a pony,
and had a big square head
and a black face with a brown patch
over one eye.
His left ear looked okay, as ears go,
but his right ear bent in the middle
and flopped up and down when he ran.
He didn't run much anymore.

Herbert said Orville was too big and too wild
to run free, so they chained him to the barn.
Maybelle said it was too cruel
to just leave him there,
through all kinds of days and all kinds of seasons,
but Herbert was firm
and Maybelle was busy,
and besides, her heart was broken.
So Orville lay in the shade
and ate his food and slept
and dreamed.

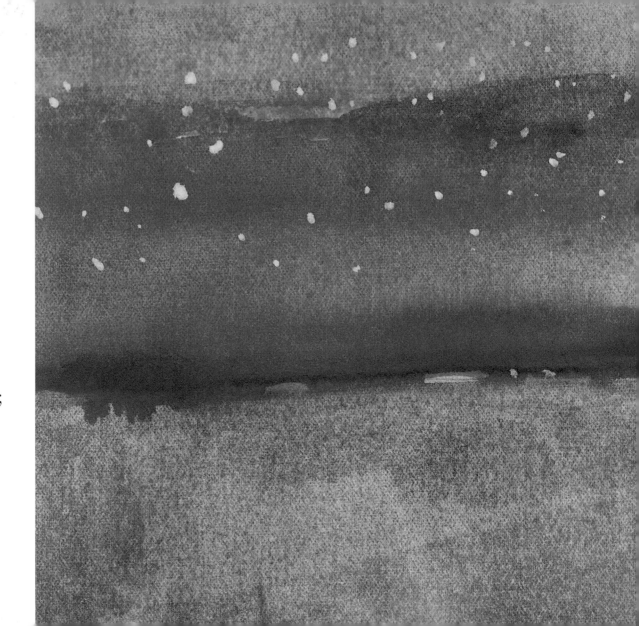

At night he could smell the stars coming out.
He looked up and saw a big dog
and a little dog, the way they ran
in a sky that was darker than the dark barn
and wider than the fields behind him.
He smelled the hoot owl jump from her perch;
he smelled the rabbits sleeping.
He thought of the field behind the house,
the deer that ran so fast
they seemed to be flying.
He knew he had nowhere to go.

Night after night, Orville thought
about the world, and all his sadness
turned angry. He knew about the broken
hearts of people, and how they failed
to love or do right, and knowing
what he knew just made him want to bark.
He took to barking.

When Herbert brought him breakfast
in the morning,
Orville barked and barked
and pulled on his chain.
When May came out to check his water,
Orville barked and barked
and threw himself against his chain
until she became too afraid
to get close to him, and sometimes
for a whole day all Orville had
in his water pan was a chunk of ice
with bits of straw mixed in.

Every day he grew angrier and angrier,
and then at night when he first smelled
the moon, Orville would lie down sadly
and think what an awful, lonesome life
his had turned out to be.
And the dog stars would run across the sky,
and by morning even those would be gone,
and as they disappeared, he would wonder
what had ever become of his mother,
or the brother he had loved the best.
And then it would be time to start barking.

Herbert said, "If you keep barking like this,
we'll take you to the pound."
Maybelle said, "You're leaving us no choice."
Orville barked and barked against his chain.
And right in the middle of a long summer day,
when he had barked about how
he was really a good dog in a bad mood,
about how he missed that one-eyed doll,
about how there was something
so terrible about the feeling of a chain
against a neck, everything changed,
because a girl with cotton-candy hair
moved into the little house across the road
and Orville fell in love.

He ran out to the very end of his chain
and watched the girl get out of an old
pickup truck. In the back he could see
a battered wing chair,
a reading lamp,
a red telephone,
a sofa that smelled decidedly like a horse,
and a box of clothes.
The girl's hair was yellow-white
and was piled up on top of her head.
She was a half-starved thing, Orville noticed,
so that her hair looked like cotton candy
on a stick.

He looked as long as he could look,
and then he began to bark.
He pulled on his chain until his eyes
nearly popped, and then he barked
and pulled some more.
May came to the window and said,
"Hush!"
and Herbert looked up
from where he was working on a tractor
half a mile down the road and said,
"Stupid dog."
And the girl across the road
looked at Orville
and raised her arm in a wave,
and this is what he smelled:

Her name was Sally Macintosh.
She worked the midnight shift
in the box factory.
She had dark circles under her eyes,
wrote with her left hand,
and hadn't seen her parents
in more than two years.
She was as alone as a person can figure out
how to be, and she wished:
To visit a county fair.
To learn to knit a sweater.
To be loved, just once in her life.

Nights now, Orville watched Sally Macintosh
climb in the truck and head off to work,
and when she came home in the morning,
he didn't bark.
He worried about his chain.
The dog stars came and went,
and Orville made a plan.

It was Friday, and May left to go visiting.
Herbert was working.
Sally Macintosh was asleep.
Orville pulled this way and that,
harder this way, harder that,
and with one final tug that nearly broke
his good ear,
he slid out of his chain and ran silently
across the road.
He felt like a deer running over a field.

He nosed open the screen door.
Sally was asleep on the horsehair sofa.
For a moment Orville could only stand still
and listen, and watch Sally's hair
cloud out on the pillow
like spilled milk.
He lay down quietly on the floor
in front of the couch
and just before he fell asleep, too,
Orville smelled what Sally was dreaming:
A hill covered with purple flowers.
A woman waiting at the bottom
with a birthday cake.

Sally woke up to see May at the screen door.
They had never met before,
and Sally was confused.
"Can I help you?" she asked.
And May pointed at the floor,
where Orville was lying, just waking.
May said, "I followed his paw prints."
Sally was so frightened
she covered her mouth with her hand,
and a noise came out
that sounded like "Mmmfff!"
And Orville thought Sally was in trouble,
and so he started barking.
And his bark was very, very big
inside the little house.

25

Maybelle said, "I'll go find Herbert," and left,
but Sally didn't know who Herbert was,
so she reached out slowly
and picked up the red telephone
and called the volunteer fire department.
And within minutes
the big red fire truck was tearing
down the country road, raising dust.
The firemen drove into Sally's lane so fast
they bumped into a small tree
and left a hole in the small yard,
and then they all jumped out of the truck at once
and started pulling off the giant
hoses and ladders.
And what Orville saw
was a bunch of strange men in rubber coats,
and then he really started to bark.

Sally yelled, "I'm not on fire!"
And the fireman in front shouted
to the firemen in back, "There's no fire!"
And before they could figure out
why they were there,
Herbert strolled in and took Orville
by the good ear and led him out,
leaving the firemen to ponder
what they ought to do next.

Herbert said, "That's it for this old dog.
I'll take him to the pound tomorrow."
And May nodded, but she was sad to see him go.
And Orville was placed back on his chain,
and Friday went on like Friday,
except the dog lay very still
and watched Sally's door,
and Sally lay wakeful,
thinking about her life, and about
what a really ugly dog he was,
but how there had been something about him,
some crooked-eared thing
that made her a little homesick . . .
for what, she couldn't say.

And on Saturday, as soon as he could,
Orville again slipped from his chain
and slid into Sally's house,
and again he guarded her while she slept,
and the firemen were called,
and Herbert took him by the ear,
but it was too late for the pound
and so he was spared another day.
And that night the stars smelled like jasmine
and mown clover,
and if Orville had found a harmonica,
and if he'd known what a harmonica was,
he would have picked it up
and given it a toot,
just like that.

On Sunday, when Sally Macintosh
woke to see the huge and ugly dog asleep
on the floor for the third time,
she reached for the red telephone.
Across the road May and Herbert's eyes met,
and the volunteer fire department
drove slowly into Sally's lane,
and the first fireman off the truck—
Jimmy Duncan, who'd never had a girlfriend
because of the way his ears stuck out
and his hair stuck up—
said sweetly to Sally,
"Ma'am, I think the dog just *loves* you."
And Sally looked at Orville
and said, "Oh."

Late that summer, when August
was nearly gone, Sally entered Orville
in the Ugliest Dog contest at the county fair,
and Orville won. First prize
was the chance to lead the fair parade
in a big green tractor with a radio in the cab,
and Sally, just guessing, thought
May and Herbert might enjoy it
more than she would.
So the two of them
led the parade down Broad Street,
with Orville sitting between them,
while Sally and Jimmy Duncan waved
from the crowd.

Sometimes Maybelle came to visit Sally
and brought a cake,
shaking her head and saying,
"Look at the two of you."
And Orville wished he could say to people,
"There are ways to slip free of a chain."
But all he could do was watch them:
Maybelle, who had no sister and no daughter
but could knit a sweater.
Sally, who had no mother
and was cold all winter.
Herbert, dozing fitfully in his chair
by the window.
It would all work out somehow, Orville guessed,
and he scratched at his neck
where there was no chain,
and sighed,
and smelled the night coming on.